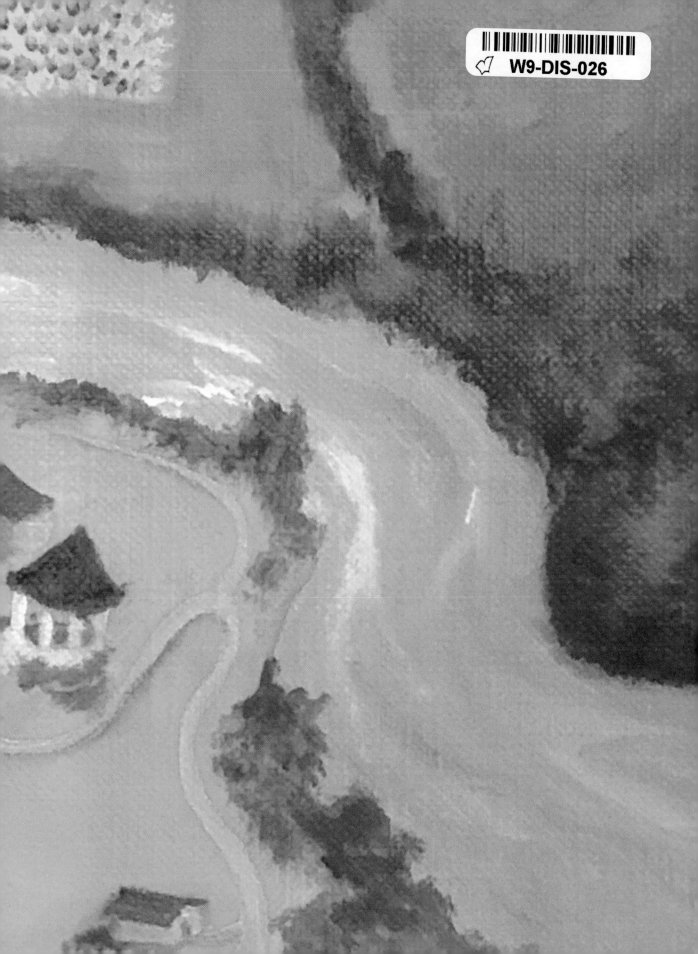

Book design by Tyler McCabe. Find him at *tylermccabe.co*

In the spirit of the Seventh Story, we'd love you to share the message of this book as widely as possible. We would be grateful if you would point people to
theseventhstory.com and *theporchmagazine.com,*
as well as the authors' and illustrator's websites:
brianmclaren.net,
garethhiggins.net,
and *heatherlynnharris.com*

Printed in Canada

First Printing, 2018

ISBN 978-1-7329437-0-4

www.theseventhstory.com

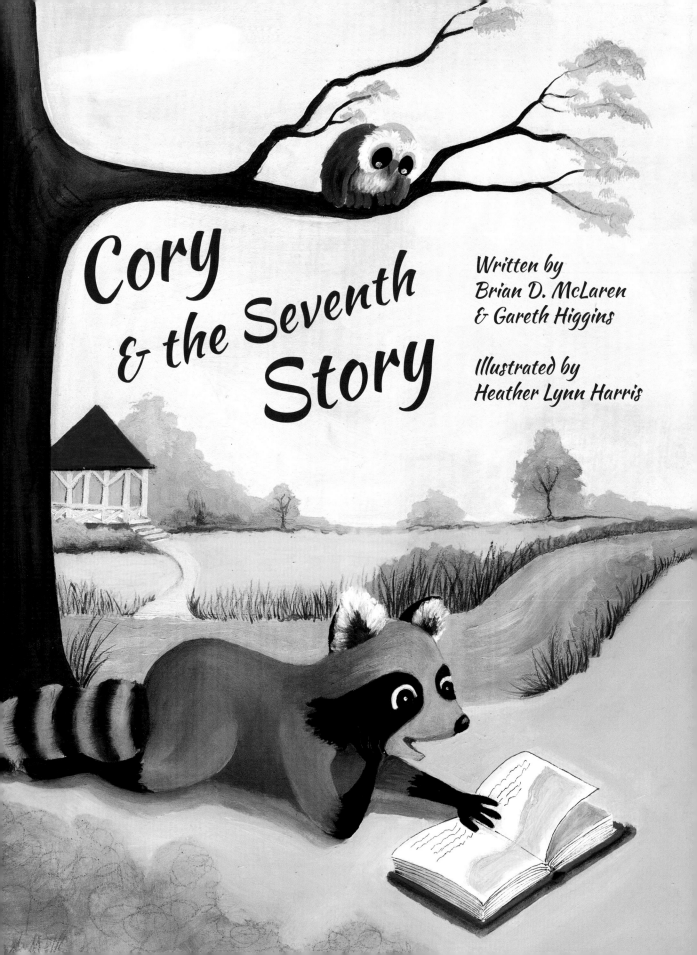

Cory & the Seventh Story

Written by
Brian D. McLaren
& Gareth Higgins

Illustrated by
Heather Lynn Harris

To my five grandchildren: Averie, Ella, Mia, Lucas, and Ada. I hope the seventh story guides your life.

–Brian

To the friends who enlarge my circle of belonging, courage, and reconciliation, and especially Brian Ammons.

–Gareth

To my mother — for sending me to art class when I was five years old.

–Heather

There once was a young raccoon named Cory.

Cory lived in the Old Village, along the clear stream, near the deep forest, within the broad meadow.

Cory loved stories. Stories about long ago . . . stories about today . . . stories about someday in the future. Most of all, Cory loved stories that end "happily ever after."

Every morning, Cory woke up full of excitement for the day's adventures: climbing trees, crossing creeks, and exploring new places with Owl, Cory's best friend.

One day, Cory went on a walk through the Old Village.

Owl, as usual, flew along.

The young raccoon saw Fox and Badger fighting. They snarled and screeched. They scratched and bit. Finally, Fox ran away in defeat, and Badger turned to Cory.

"You like stories, so here is mine," he growled. "Fox had a shiny object. I wanted it, so I took it. Now everyone will be afraid of me, so I can take whatever I want. I'll take over Old Village just like our ancestors did when they pushed the first residents away. I will rule by tooth and claw over the Old Village and I will live happily ever after!"

From that day forward, Badger started pushing everyone around to get his own way. He took whatever he wanted.

Everyone in the Old Village was afraid of him and very, very sad. "Poor us!" they said. "Life is so unfair!"

"Who, who, who will help us?" cried Owl.

The next day, Cory saw Fox whispering to her friend, Weasel.

"What are you talking about?" Cory asked.

"We have a plan," Weasel whispered. "We are going to get revenge on that bad Badger!"

Fox and Weasel quickly formed a mob of angry neighbors. Then they marched through town looking for Badger.

When they found Badger, they surrounded him. Soon the sounds of fighting, yelling, scratching, punching, growling, whacking, and snapping echoed through the Old Village. When the fight was over, Fox and Weasel were in power.

From that day forward, Badger had to do whatever Fox and Weasel said.

"Our enemy is defeated!" Fox and Weasel shouted with joy. "Now we will live happily ever after!"

Fox and Weasel were no better than Badger. They ruled the Old Village by tooth and claw. They made everyone afraid and took whatever they wanted. Nobody felt safe.

"Different rulers, but the same danger!" Owl said to Cory. "Who, who, who will help us?"

Just then, Rabbit hopped, skipped, and jumped up to Cory and Owl. She ran fast circles around them as she spoke in her high-pitched voice. "The Old Village is a mess!" she said. "There's fighting and trouble everywhere!"

Then she stopped suddenly, perking up her ears. "I know what to do," she said, speaking very quickly. "Whenever there's danger, run away fast!"

So Rabbit sped away to share her idea with others. "Hurry! Let's go!" she said.

She convinced many neighbors to run away with her. They hopped, flew, jumped, and scampered through the broad meadow and crossed over the clear stream. They built a new neighborhood on the other side. They even put up a great big wall to keep everyone else out.

"Now we will live happily ever after!" Rabbit squealed.

A few weeks later, Cory and Owl went to visit them.

"What's new? What's your story?" Cory asked. "Are you living happily ever after?"

"No, no, no, we're not happy at all!" Rabbit said. "We moved to a new place, but we brought our old stories with us!"

"Some of us are acting like Badger, ruling over others. Some are acting like Fox and Weasel, making plans to overthrow the rulers. Now we are even worse off than before, trapped behind this great big wall! Life is so unfair!" Rabbit said, hardly taking a breath.

Then she blinked three times, and a big tear formed in her right eye and moved slowly down her face. "We jumped from one mess into another! What can we do now?" Rabbit asked, her lips quivering.

"Maybe you should come back to the Old Village with us," Cory said. "Then we can work on our problems together."

Rabbit's eyes brightened. She jumped up, hopped away, and quickly convinced the others to return to the Old Village.

When they arrived, Old Skunk was standing on a stump, giving a speech to a crowd in Old Village Square.

"You know what's wrong with this village?" Old Skunk asked. "We have been invaded by animals who don't fit in! Normal folks in this village have fur or feathers, but the invaders are different. They have . . . yucky scales or slimy skin!"

Nobody had noticed this before. They shoved Turtle, Lizard, Snake, and Frog into the center of the circle in front of Old Skunk.

He pointed a sharp claw at them and growled.

Soon everyone was pointing at them, laughing at them, and making jokes about the way they looked.

"Don't you think Old Village would be a better place if we cleaned it up and got those dirty, disgusting invaders out of here?" Old Skunk snarled.

Suddenly, the crowd started shoving Turtle, Lizard, Snake, and Frog to the edge of town. "This is OUR Village," the crowd shouted. "You're not welcome here anymore!"

Turtle, Lizard, Snake, and Frog were surprised and hurt to see their neighbors reject them. They escaped into the deep forest to hide. "Life is so unfair!" they whispered, partly to themselves and partly to each other.

Cory was upset and walked up to Old Skunk and said, "Why were you so mean to our neighbors?"

"When people are worried or afraid," Old Skunk hissed, "you just have to give them somebody different to blame for their problems. If they call somebody else dirty or bad, they will feel clean and good. If they hurt somebody who won't hurt them back, they will feel very powerful, important, and safe. It works every time."

"But that's wrong!" Cory said.

Old Skunk stepped back and looked at Cory from head to toe. He said, "Have you ever noticed that most folks in this village don't have a mask or a ringed tail?"

Old Skunk showed his sharp teeth, and Cory wasn't sure if he was smiling or snarling.

The next day, Cory went for a walk and noticed something really strange. Almost everyone was wearing baggy gray coats. And nobody smiled and said hello. They just walked quickly down the street, looking as if they were in a hurry . . . and a little bit worried.

When Porcupine walked by, Cory stopped him.

"What's going on here?" Cory asked. "Why are you covering up what makes you special?"

Porcupine looked around nervously and then whispered, "I don't want Old Skunk to see my quills. I'm afraid he will laugh at me and then I will have to go hide in the forest. Skunk has ruined everything for everyone. Now we will have to wear these ugly coats for the rest of our lives. There's nothing we can do about it." He shook his head and rushed quickly away.

Cory's neighbors lived in a gray world of sameness and fear. "Life is so unfair!" they cried, feeling very sorry for themselves.

"Who, who, who will help us?" Owl asked.

That's when Badger remembered something.

He remembered how happy he was when he first stole the shiny object from Fox. He went to talk to her.

"We could make everyone happy," he said, "if we sold everyone shiny objects! And we could get very rich too!"

So Badger and Fox built a shiny object factory. Soon everybody in the Old Village was buying shiny objects. They wore shiny objects as jewelry. They played with shiny objects as toys. They put shiny objects on their houses and used them to decorate their baggy gray coats.

"Who has the most shiny objects?" Mouse asked.

"Who has the biggest shiny object?" Deer wondered.

"Who has the most money from making and selling shiny objects to everyone?" Fox and Badger asked, laughing, because they knew the answer.

After that, Cory heard neighbors telling shiny object stories everywhere. "Just a few more shiny objects," they said, "and we will live happily ever after!"

Cory wanted to believe them. But, looking around, Cory didn't feel happy.

Badger and Fox cut down many beautiful trees to burn as fuel for their shiny object factory.

The smokestacks filled the air with smelly gray smoke.

The shiny object factory dumped dirty water onto the ground, and it flowed into the clear stream where the fish and tadpoles lived.

Whenever there was a sports event or a concert, someone would interrupt with annoying shiny object commercials.

And ugly SHINY OBJECTS! BIG SALE! signs were popping up everywhere.

Cory walked alone to the clear stream to sit by the water and think.

"We are in trouble," Cory thought. "Our stories are failing us. No one will live happily ever after in a world like this."

Owl flew over to perch in a nearby tree.

They didn't say a word as they watched the water flow by and listened to its gentle music.

Cory leaned over, looked down into the clear water, and saw a sad raccoon face looking back.

Suddenly, another face appeared.

It was a large face with big brown eyes, a majestic creature that Cory had never seen before.

"Wh-wh-what are you?" Cory asked, still staring at the reflection in the water. "Are you a monster?"

"I am a horse. My name is Swift."

With that, Swifthorse bent down to take a drink from the clear stream, just inches away from Cory.

Cory's head slowly turned to take in the amazing creature: her pointed ears, her long sleek neck, her tall shoulders, her strong legs, her wide back, her coffee-brown coat, her long, flowing black tail.

"I've never seen a horse before," Cory said. "What is your story, Swifthorse?"

"I am a poet from far away," Swifthorse said. "I travel the world seeking wisdom and beauty, and I share what I find in well-chosen words."

"I am happy to meet you," Cory said. "I need wisdom and beauty because I have a very big problem and the world feels very ugly to me right now."

Swifthorse lowered her head and pointed her ears toward the young raccoon. Their noses were almost touching.

"Tell me," she said.

"My neighbors are living by stories that will only bring fighting, tears, and trouble," Cory said.

Then Cory told Swifthorse about Badger taking power . . . Fox and Weasel taking revenge . . . Rabbit running away with some villagers . . . Old Skunk scaring away other villagers . . . Porcupine and the baggy gray coats . . . the rise of the shiny object factory . . . and all of Cory's sad neighbors who felt that life was so unfair.

For a long time, Swifthorse listened to Cory, breathing in long, slow breaths. When Cory finished speaking, Owl called out from the tree above them. You know what she said.

"Who, who, who will help us?"

Swifthorse answered, "Maybe it's time for you to look within for the help you need. I have a plan. Climb on my back and I will explain."

Cory scampered up the tree and dropped onto Swifthorse's back, and Owl joined Cory there. As they trotted along, Swifthorse shared her plan.

When they reached Old Village Square, a crowd quickly gathered because no one had ever seen a creature so large and so beautiful as Swifthorse.

"Let's have a special meal in honor of our special guest," Cory said. "Let's set up a big round table, and let's all bring our favorite food to share. But please, everyone, please leave your shiny objects at home."

While their neighbors prepared the special meal, Cory and Owl rode Swifthorse out into the deep forest. They found Turtle, Lizard, Snake, and Frog and invited them home. As the sun was setting, they returned to the Old Village, riding on Swifthorse's back.

They saw the big round table full of delicious food. Cory gave the furless, featherless neighbors the places of greatest honor, right next to Swifthorse.

Then Cory asked everyone to take off their baggy grey coats so Swifthorse could see their beautiful, wonderful differences.

As they ate their meal, Cory's neighbors told their stories, stories from their own lives and stories from the long-ago days of their ancestors, stories of hope and joy, stories of pain and sorrow. Swifthorse listened carefully to every word.

After the meal, Cory turned to Swifthorse. "Would you recite one of your poems for us?"

She nodded her head, shook her mane, looked at each guest with her big brown eyes, and began to speak. Her gentle, strong voice sounded like a song.

Six old stories, wherever I go,

The same six stories are running the show:

The story of power to dominate,

The story of striking back with fury and hate,

The story of running to find a safe place,

Or pointing at others to shame and disgrace,

Or being stuck in self-pity for the pain we've been through,

Or of me having more shiny objects than you.

These same six old stories steal freedom and laughter,

So nobody lives happily ever after. But . . .

Swifthorse began walking around the table as she continued her poem, her hooves clip-clopping to the rhythm of her words.

There's a new Seventh Story to live by, my friends,

A new Seventh Story without "us against them"—

Of working for fairness in all that we do,

Of refusing to strike back when others strike you,

Of facing our problems and not running to hide,

Of not letting differences make us divide,

Of turning our pain into compassion for others,

Of not wanting more than our sisters and brothers.

The new Seventh Story that I'm speaking of

Is the story of peace, and the hero is love.

For a long, long time, there was only the sound of the wind in the trees and Swifthorse's hooves as she circled the big round table.

Swifthorse stopped walking and spoke again: "My friends, the most wonderful story in the universe is the story of love growing and spreading from one heart to another. We all get to play a part in this story."

"There is no big or small, no short or tall,
No best or worst, no blessed or cursed,
No dirty or clean, no cause to be mean,
No rich or poor, no reason for war,
We have more than enough in the story of love.
Each is for all of us, and all are for each of us.
This is the wisdom this new story teaches us."

Eyes blinked and opened wide. Ears perked up, tails twitched, brows furrowed, and feathers ruffled. All around the table, faces looked surprised and curious. Smiles began to form on many faces. Swifthorse raised her head and let out a loud whinny that echoed through the streets.

Nobody had ever heard about a Seventh Story before. It sounded beautiful and wise to nearly everyone.

Except for Badger, Fox, Weasel, and Skunk. All at once, they started growling and snarling, growling and snarling.

"No! Stop! Be quiet! You're hurting our ears with your words!" they shouted. "Go back to where you came from! We like ruling over others by tooth and by claw. We like wearing our baggy grey coats! And most of all, we like making more and more money by selling more and more shiny objects. We will never, ever, EVER have enough! And we will never, ever, EVER live by your silly Seventh Story. Go away, and never come back, you big ugly donkey!"

Badger, Fox, Weasel, and Skunk started throwing leftover food at Swifthorse, and then they threw their plates and silverware too. They snarled terrible words at her. She began walking away, and then turned back, her eyes so sad, yet so full of love. In her gentle but strong voice, she said:

Drive the poet away, but this story will stay.
Long after I'm gone, the story lives on.

Her words only made them more angry. They jumped up from the table, ran toward her, and snapped at her legs. They drove her out of the village, over the broad meadow, and to the edge of the clear stream near the deep forest, snarling and growling and snapping all the way.

Nobody knows for sure what happened to Swifthorse after that. Some say they hurt her. Some say they did something even worse. Whatever happened, Swifthorse has never again been seen in the Old Village.

Since that day, Badger and Fox have been getting richer and richer, selling shiny objects. The sky is getting smoky and the stream is getting murky because of the shiny object factory. Old Skunk still says terrible things about neighbors without fur or feathers. Many feel life is very, very unfair.

But Swifthorse's Seventh Story is still alive in many hearts, which means that a surprise is coming. Late in the day as the sun is setting, you can find more and more animals walking out of the Old Village to the stream to talk with Cory and Owl about the Seventh Story.

Fox even joins them sometimes.

They leave their shiny objects home. They take off their baggy gray coats and let their beautiful differences show. They recite Swifthorse's poem, and they all bring food and share a meal.

They build a glowing fire and sit in a circle around it.

After a while, Cory knows it's time to speak.

"Swifthorse was right," Cory says. "The old stories separate the Old Village into us and them."

"Us ruling over them,
us overthrowing them,
us getting away from them,
us bullying and rejecting them,
us feeling sorry for ourselves because of them, or
us having more shiny objects than them."

"But this is the truth," Cory says. "There is no *them*. We are all part of one great, big, beautiful, wonderful *us*."

"We can all choose to be a part of a healing story: the story of love. This story can set us free. This story can lead to a happy ending for everyone."

"Who, who, who will choose the Seventh Story of love?" Owl asks.

Then Cory looks each person in the eye, just as Swifthorse did, so full of love, and asks three simple questions.

"Which stories are you living by lately?
How are they working out for you?
How can we live the Seventh Story together?"

They sit around the fire and talk late into the night. ✦

A Letter from Us to the Rest of Us

Dearest Rest of Us,

In one of Brian's fondest memories as a boy in upstate New York, he's sitting with his dad on a 1950s-style couch reading a story. Fast-forward thirty years and he's sitting on a 1980s-style couch reading stories with his kids. Then zip to the present, and you'll find one or more of his five grandkids crowded in his lap, and they're still sharing the joy of reading stories across generations.

Gareth still finds his imagination nurtured by the Shakespearean tales and cinematic narratives his parents introduced him to growing up in Belfast.

And Heather remembers with a smile listening to her dad tell stories and recite poems for the family around the campfire in Rochester, NY.

However, we didn't write *Cory and the Seventh Story* only for kids. In fact, it began as a "children's book for adults" because the ideas in it are so radical that grown-ups have often forgotten them. Only an appeal to childlike wonder might be enough to remind us of what we used to know. Kids—and adults, when we open our minds—will instinctively recognize the seven stories found in this book:

1. Being the boss of others
2. Getting revenge on those who bossed you around

3. Running away afraid
4. Turning on those who look different
5. Giving up in helplessness
6. Taking pride in having more than others

And, seventh, ultimately finding joy in belonging to a great, big, beautiful, hospitable Us.

As you read this book with your loved ones, think about the stories we all live by.

Ask questions about how the six stories in the Old Village resemble Us-versus-Them stories you see playing out at home, at school, among friends, and in current events.

Domination: Us Ruling Over Them
Revolution: Us Overthrowing Them
Isolation: Us Apart from Them
Purification: Us Marginalizing or Excluding Them
Victimization: Us Defeated by Them
Accumulation: Us With More Than Them

And the Seventh Story, which is Reconciliation: us and them learning to be in right relationship, creating a bigger, all-inclusive us. Us for them, or even better, *some of us for all of us.*

More and more of us are coming to believe that the Seventh Story is the best way to live, whatever our age, gender, race, religion, politics, or nationality.

You may say that we are dreamers, but we're not the only ones!

In fact, each time the old stories of oppression, revenge, withdrawal, marginalization, despair, and greed seem to make a comeback, this Seventh Story rises up in creative resistance, with even more resilience than before, alive afresh in new faces, new voices, new movements, new generations, and new ways of understanding the human story. We are part of a Seventh Story movement, and by stepping into the ideas in this book, you are too. If you'd like to join in, learn more, and find additional resources, check out *theseventhstory.com*.

And you can find more about us at *brianmclaren.net, garethhiggins.net*, and *heatherlynnharris.com*.

Thank you for reading.

In the fellowship of the Seventh Story,

> *Heather Harris,*
> *Gareth Higgins,*
> *& Brian D. McLaren*

Notes & Drawings

We're grateful to many friends who helped with the shaping of the ideas in this book, and we look forward to continued conversations and experiments in the Seventh Story.